Conversation of the Three Wayfarers

Conversation of the Three Wayfarers

Peter Weiss

translated from the German by E. B. Garside
with an introduction by John Keene

A NEW DIRECTIONS PAPERBOOK

Originally published as *Das Gespräch der drei Gehenden* by Suhrkamp Verlag
in 1963

First published as New Directions Paperbook 1528 in 2022
Manufactured in the United States of America

Library of Congress Cataloging-in-Publication Data
Names: Weiss, Peter, 1916–1982, author. | Garside, E. B. (Edward Ballard),
1907–1999, translator. | Keene, John, 1965– other.
Title: The conversation of the three wayfarers / Peter Weiss ; translated
from the German by E. B. Garside ; with an introduction by John Keene.
Other titles: Gespräch der drei Gehenden. English
Description: New York : New Directions Publishing Corporation, 2022.
Identifiers: LCCN 2021057647 | ISBN 9780811231633 (paperback) |
ISBN 9780811231640 (ebook)
Subjects: LCGFT: Novels.
Classification: LCC PT2685.E5 G4513 2022 | DDC 833/.914—dc23/eng/20211203
LC record available at https://lccn.loc.gov/2021057647

10 9 8 7 6 5 4 3 2 1

New Directions Books are published for James Laughlin
by New Directions Publishing Corporation
80 Eighth Avenue, New York 10011

Introduction

If the name Peter Weiss (1916–1982) sparks any recognition at all these days, it is likely because of his authorship of one of the major theater works of the late twentieth century, the formally experimental, philosophically and politically profound *Marat/Sade* (Full title: *The Persecution and Assassination of Jean-Paul Marat as Performed by the Inmates of the Asylum of Charenton under the Direction of the Marquis de Sade*), his play-within-a-play that was first staged in 1964 in Berlin. Weiss's acclaim as a playwright continued with a host of works that included his 1965 work *The Investigation: Oratorio in 11 Cantos*, a documentary treatment of the Frankfurt Auschwitz trials, and his adaptation and revision of Franz Kafka's *The Trial* (in 1974 and again with *The New Trial* in 1982). From the beginning of his multifaceted career, which included painting, filmmaking, and criticism, Weiss showed immense talent and aesthetic daring, not least in fiction, producing numerous works of fiction that culminated in his remarkable magnum opus, the three-volume (1975, 1978, 1981), thousand-page, anti-fascist novel *The Aesthetics of Resistance,* the last part of which was published a year before his death.

A native of Nowawes, in Brandenburg State, near Berlin, Germany, Weiss was the son of a Christian mother and a Hungarian Jewish father, a textile manufacturer who eventually took Czech nationality after the dissolution of the Austro-Hungarian Empire at the end of World War I. The family moved around repeatedly during his youth, residing in Bremen; in Berlin during his adolescence, where they were subject to Nazi persecution; in Chislehurst, near London; in Prague, until after Hitler's invasion of the Czech Sudetenland in 1938; and finally in Stockholm, Sweden, where Weiss landed in 1939 and would remain for the rest of his life. Though he issued several early works in Swedish, he published nearly all of his major works after 1950 in German. A figure of the political and cultural Left, Weiss's personal and artistic stances increasingly united in the 1960s when he joined the German-language Gruppe 47 and publicly opposed the Vietnam War, denouncing the United States' role in the war during a 1966 Gruppe 47 visit to the United States, and going so far as to travel to North Vietnam in 1968. Weiss would draw upon this activism and these experiences for his 1968 play *Viet Nam Discourse* (full title: *Discourse on the Progress of the Prolonged War of Liberation in Viet Nam and the Events Leading Up to It as Illustration of the Necessity for Armed Resistance against Oppression and on the Attempts of the United States of America to Destroy the Foundations of Revolution*) and for the critical text *Notes on the Cultural Life of the Democratic Republic of Vietnam*, published that same year.

The novella *Conversation of the Three Wayfarers*, whose comparatively brief title closely approximates the German original, occupies a curious place in this oeuvre. Published originally in 1962, it is neither overtly autobiographical, like several of the longer fictional works that immediately preceded it, nor evidently political, like the plays that would secure his international fame. Instead, *Conversation of the Three Wayfarers* is a quasi-fabular transitional text that stylistically somewhat harkens back to Weiss's early experiments in film and fiction, with light touches of Surrealist juxtaposition and repetition, and Brechtian techniques of defamiliarization. It is more straightforward in some ways— and less in others—than Weiss's acclaimed *The Shadow of the Coachman's Body* (1960), which established his name in German-language literature. Additionally, *Conversation of the Three Wayfarers* hints at the social and political critiques that would underpin his writings, particularly his plays, which contributed so much to the Theater of Fact or Documentary Theater movement in the years to follow.

Rather, this novella reads like the working out of an abstracted idea: instead of the form the title suggests (a conversation or dialogue), the text proceeds in a refracted manner with no discernible plot or clear arc, and it is unclear throughout most of the narrative *who* is actually speaking, though *what* the speaker or speakers conveys unreels in an almost incantatory fashion that holds the reader's attention while gradually indicating *how* one might assemble this puzzle into a coherent whole.

If Weiss's earlier works reflect a Modernist approach to form, time, and other elements of fiction, *Conversation of the Three Wayfarers* anticipates the postmodern in its abrupt shifts between contemporaneity—with mentions of fluorescent lights, traffic, and factory buildings—and its dreamlike elision of chronological time or any fixed locations at all. One way to understand Weiss's storytelling here is to view it as a roundabout way of describing a Germany, and a Europe for that matter, after the upheavals of various world wars (particularly World War II), the Holocaust, and the capitalist onslaught that followed. The text suggests a particular moment in time and yet stands jarringly outside it. The old fables or stories, it seems to say, will not suffice, but the new ones must struggle toward coherence.

The three figures we are introduced to at the novella's opening, Abel, Babel and Cabel, are clearly (at least the first two) biblically named; the exact rhyming of the names suggests an element of absurdity. Much like their rhyming monikers, the text that follows does almost nothing to distinguish these three by character traits, actions, or any other means. Moreover, we never know whether Abel, Babel, or Cabel is relating the stories to us, since there are no quotes or shifts in voice or tone to mark out any of the trio. They are both multiple and the same. As we proceed, however, we may grasp that the point of this novella is not for each of our wanderers (whose tales initially wander all over the place) to tell individual stories that collectively paint a portrait of an era, in the manner, for example, of *Billiards at Half Past Nine* (1958), a novel by Weiss's exact contemporary Heinrich Böll, but rather that each of these amblers through an unfocused present bears the various traumas of modernity, particularly European modernity, from industrialization to war to mass murder, that their accounts, sometimes repetitious, sometimes verging on the phasmagorical, fragmentarily impart.

When the novella introduces the six semiarchetypal, fantastical sons of the ferryman—Jam, Jem, Jim, Jom, Jum, and Jym—it is clear that we are beyond the vale of realism, and that depicting a realist social, political, and economic picture here is not Weiss's goal. Put another way, instead of depicting the changes to this world through a conventional fictional approach, Weiss captures the psychological and material reality of the disorientation, the dispossession, and the disruption that pre- and postwar capital, as well as World War II itself and its aftermath, have wrought. The narrator or narrators show the effects of this through a series of observations and recollections, such as the ferryman's loss of his job and key societal role once the new bridge is erected, or the speaker's experience of having to hide at the edge of the town (for reasons we can only guess at), or watching the arrival of a military column proceeding down the street. It is a circuitous method, but by the novella's end, an effective one.

Abel, Babel, and Cabel keep walking, and talking, or someone is walking and talking, and narrating, step-by-step, story-by-story—the "I" a we, a chorus—events and incidents, returning to key scenes involving the past, wars large and small, the ferryman, his sons, fathers and mothers, the nearby city itself, and so on, right up to the novella's end, remembering and recounting. These narrators, or conversants, are remembering the past, recounting experiences, piecing together a world that gradually begins to coalesce, filled with lives of coalescing selves moving through space and time, if not identifiable here on any fixed map then at least on an interior one, providing the reader with perhaps one of the most basic and profound truths of storytelling, which is that it is through narrative that we make sense of the world, just as Weiss's characters here—however haltingly—cumulatively succeed in doing, and thereby make what they, and we, call the past, the future, and the present (as the novel's unpunctuated, ongoing ending underscores) possible and comprehensible.

JOHN KEENE

Conversation of the Three Wayfarers

They were men who did nothing but walk walk walk. They were big, they were bearded, they wore leather caps and long raincoats, they called themselves Abel, Babel and Cabel, and while they walked they talked to each other. They walked and looked around and saw what there was to see, and they talked about it and about other things that had happened. When one was talking the two others kept still and listened or looked around and listened to something else, and when one of them had finished saying what he had to say, the second one spoke up, and then the third, and the others listened or thought about something else. They had stout boots for walking, but they carried only as much with them as would fit into the pockets of their clothes, as much as they could quickly lay their hands on and put away again. Since they looked alike they were taken for brothers by passersby, but they were not brothers at all, they were only men who walked walked walked, having met each other by chance, Abel and Babel, and then Abel, Babel and Cabel. Abel and Babel had met each other on the bridge, Babel, who had been coming toward Abel, turned round and joined company with Abel, and Cabel ran into them in the park and since then they walked walked walked everywhere together.

I believe this bridge is a new one, I have never seen it before, it must have been built overnight, a difficult job requiring long preparation and a great expenditure of effort. Pontoons were towed in and barges with planks, the pontoons were anchored, the planks set in place and lagged fast, after careful calculations and with the help of a selected workforce. Master-builder, engineers, workmen, members of the city administration knew months ahead about the bridge, when people were still calling to each other from the open banks. At that time rowboats traveled back and forth through the rapids, also a flat open ferry. Have often crossed on the ferry, the trip an interval of standing still and despite that of moving forward, on the blue water, under clouds and seagulls. The ferry engine puffed, vibrations came up through the deck into the soles of your shoes, up your legs, into the body, as in regular quick walking. The ferryman's face was covered with shining white stubble, his skin was darkly tanned and covered with lines and furrows. He lived in a shack over there on the bank, near the pile to which the ferry lay tied up. During the crossings I talked with him, his words were unclear because he always had a pipe held between his teeth, a short sturdy pipe wound with wire and insulating tape. In our most recent conversation he seemed not to have known about the projected bridge. If I understood him correctly he foresaw a long future for himself on his pounding, wave-cleaving ferry, in the blue air, in wind and in rain, and many planks had gone into putting the ferry together, and many nights in his shack, with the view through the window of the pile with the tautly stretched hawser. It is possible that he had built the ferry himself in his early years, not alone, but with the help of other boatbuilders, perhaps he was only a helper, in any case he knew how many planks had gone into putting the ferry together, and how many ribs and bolts had been needed for its completion. It had often been repaired and tarred since then, nonetheless water steadily leaked in, every morning he had to pump out. When the tower clock on the castle struck out another full hour he traveled from the bank where his shack lay across to the other bank, no matter whether any ferry passengers had come aboard or not, or whether any passengers were waiting on the other side. He came back the same way from the other bank and if people came running from afar he did not wait and the people over there could shout and whistle as much as they liked, he came back only when the hour had run out again.

The bridge has existed for a long time. I was riding one time in a black lacquered, redly upholstered coach over the bridge and next to me sat my bride and vomited on her white dress because the bridge swayed on the pontoons and the sections of the roadway rose and fell. The coachman in front of us up on the driver's seat just lifted his whip, which was decorated with a white ribbon, and the horse lost his footing, buckled at the knees and remained prostrate in a confusion of harness. From the impact of the vehicle behind us, in which my bride's parents were sitting, we were thrown forward, a bursting of wood could be heard, a neighing, a thunder of hooves, and the other horse, which had torn itself loose, broke into a gallop between the lines of autos, a gray horse speckled all over with red, like the bridal veil that was fluttering out of the window. One of the shafts of the coach behind us had punched through our conveyance and its splintered point stuck out through the upholstery. The coachman ran after the runaway horse, his woolen waterproof flapping, swinging his whip, and the occupants of the automobiles that had come to a stop stuck out their heads. The fallen horse lay on his side, motionless, his legs stuck out stiffly from him, except for the broken foreleg, over the bloody bone-stump of which our coachman bent down. With eyes obliquely straining the horse looked up at him, his head patiently leaned on the shaft, his nostrils and ears trembling, and wavy lines and whorls shimmering through the dark brown skin about the forehead, eyes and nose. The roadway rocked, the waves rose high, the wind whistled and, under the weight of the stalled traffic and the people who had rushed up to see, the bridge sank. Policemen and firefighters arrived, the wail of the sirens audible from a distance, brought lines with them, cranes, stretchers and tools, and men in helmets and rubber coats knelt about the horse, freed it from the traces, tied it fast under the arm of the crane on the wrecker and the horse let it all be done to him, softly snuffling, a little foam at his mouth, and officials with whistles and brusque motionings with their white gloves got the traffic moving again. As the horse under the derrick was being slowly swung onto the floor of the truck he turned his head in astonishment toward the coachman, and likely saw him for the last time, and while the horse, lying on his side, was being tied down, police came this way from the park with the other, recaptured horse, which reared and the policemen hung onto him by his bridle, their legs dangling high. The shaft was pulled out of the back wall of our coach, we got in with my bride's parents, I forced myself in between them, took my bride on my lap, both coachmen harnessed the redly speckled horse between the shafts, climbed up onto the seat, held the reins pulled taut, and the coach in which we had been riding was hitched to the back of a firetruck, and thus everything was able to get rolling again, on the floating bridge, in the sea wind, under the screaming gulls. The police car led the procession, then came the red truck with the fallen horse and the men on either side, followed by the empty coach being towed, jolting along and swinging this way and that, and finally our vehicle, with two coachmen on the driver's seat, close together, in light-gray cloaks, the collars thrown back wide over their shoulders, light-gray top hats on their heads, with feather plumes on them, I believe, and while I could see nothing that was going on because my bride's veil lay over my face, we flew back in the coach with a jerk, and then it became evident that the horse, after it had left the bridge, snorting and striking sparks from the cobbles, had overtaken the men on the wrecker, and the police car, which was now moving along beside us, again sounded its siren as it proceeded. I held my bride wrapped in my arms, at my right her father leaned far out of the window, and her mother at the left leaned still farther out, yet whereas the father shouted stop, the mother screamed for us to go faster, her hat, garnished with flowers and lace, had fallen from her head, she threw herself backward and forward, her face contorted in a wild joy, with shrill shouts she spurred the horse on, and the vehicles in front of us scattered to one side, pedestrians flew from the sidewalk into the park, where a brass band was making music, and not until we got to the square, which we circled several times, did we come to a halt, after two police cars, pressing in from right and left, got the horse squeezed in between them, and this happened in front of the entrance to the hotel, where the room for the wedding night had been engaged, the porter was already standing there, ready to receive us.

Yesterday I made another trip on the ferry, and the ferryman told me about his sons, he had six sons, and this morning, as I traveled across, he told me about three of them, this evening, as I came back, he told me about the three others. The first son was small and round, I don't know whether he was the oldest, in any case he was the first to be mentioned. He had red cheeks and red hair, short fat arms and puffy hands. He held his mouth open, he had very small sharp teeth and a pointed nose, his nose was turned up and when it rained, it rained into all the openings in his face. The second son was long and thin, his eyes lay deep in their sockets, his skull was bald, his cheeks sunken in. He had only one arm, the other had been eaten away by gangrene. But with his remaining hand he could do lots of things better than many with two hands, playing skat and perhaps playing the piano, too. The third son was built like a giant, he had a coarse moustache and bristly hair, his chest was tattooed and could, when he expanded it, break an iron chain. His arms were full of scars, for he stuck needles and knives through them, and his gullet and the pit of his stomach were all beat up by swords that he stuck into them and drew out. The fourth son, according to the description, seemed to be older than the ferryman himself, which could be explained by the fact that he was a stepson whom his mother had brought along into her marriage. This son had no teeth and was able to move around only with difficulty, on crutches. When he uttered any words at all, he stammered, and nobody had the patience to hear him out. However, he always let everybody know he was there by banging a crutch on the table, and when he had been locked in the attic he banged on the floor. The fifth son was everyone's favorite. He was stout, too, much fatter than the first son. He was so fat he could scarcely move, he passed the time on the sofa, on the floor, in bed, where big pillows lay ready for him everywhere. The ferryman's eyes filled with tears when he talked about this son. He said, if I didn't misunderstand him, that he always brought him something every day when he came home from work. At that time he was still living with his family in a bigger house on the knoll beyond the bank, where the telegraph office now stands. He came home with a fish, a cherry, a snail, a cauliflower, always with something different, which he held behind his back as he came in, while the son, hearing his steps outside, impatiently wanted to know what he had brought home with him today. What did you bring me today, what have you got nice for me today, cried the ferryman in weepy mimicry, and it was one of those rare moments when he took the pipe out of his mouth. On tiptoes the ferryman would approach the place where his son was lying, meanwhile urging him to guess, and because the son always guessed wrong, the surprise was always great, and then with his own hands the ferryman would prepare the gift on the stove or the kitchen table and serve it to his son on his special plate, on the center of which was painted a dwarf with a pointed red cap. Naturally this dainty was only something special, for the mother had already cooked and spiced the main meal, yet before they all went in to eat they looked in on the bedridden son, with nods of their heads and encouraging laughs, as he ate up his hors d'oeuvre. Only the sixth son did not look on, he often had to be restrained by force by the other brothers, because he wanted to attack the fat one with a knife. The sixth son's face was of great beauty, though eaten away by the pox. He had long silky black hair that hung down to his shoulders. He wore a golden ring in his left ear and on his fingers a couple of cheap rings. He cared nothing about his clothes, they hung on his body in rags, and everywhere the yellow skin shone through. This son never slept in the house, but in a box outside in the yard which he had surrounded with barbed wire. He was big, too, but walked bent over and shambling, barefoot, or in raggedy foot-wrappings. The ferryman named names for me, too, perhaps, they were the names of his sons, and so the first was called Jam, the second Jem, the third Jim, the fourth Jom, the fifth Jum, the sixth Jym.

The bridge has been there a long time, we once rode over the bridge on the way to the registry office, a woman and I. She had come up to my place of an afternoon, I didn't recognize her again at first, had also forgotten her name, and I led her into the kitchen, her belly was sticking out. You've grown stout, I said, trying to place her, and her only answer was to smile. She sat down, sat in front of me with her legs spraddled out, held up her belly for me to see, and confidently smiled. She took hold of my hand and laid it on her belly and I felt the child moving. All the questions I asked she answered with puckerings of her lips and her belly was her only answer. I had forgotten the hours when, as she later explained to me, we had embraced in the hall to the staircase of the Academy of Science behind the guard's little cubby, under the plaster copy of the Nike of Samothrace. Imperishable hours, payment for which I was now on the way to make good before the mayor's legal counsel, and we walked into a wood-paneled room in front of a wooden rail, behind us two guards hired as witnesses, and the official knocked three times on a hollow box and looked at my future spouse's pregnant belly, and compelled us to get down on our knees on a wooden footstool, and we held fast to the wooden rail, and he read his formulas, which ticked away, hollow-sounding, in the wooden chamber, and then we wrote down our names, for all eternity, in a thick book that he held out to us.

There, I think, the ferryman just rode by, in the last car of the trolley, at the brake-wheel, he held the wheel in his hands and turned it this way and that, surely it was he standing there in the crowd, only he had such a broad-rimmed hat, so beaten up by sun and rain, only he held his short thick pipe so firmly in his mouth. After the ferry had been taken away from him, he had to find a steering wheel on the streetcars, and so he stood there, legs spread apart, his back turned toward the direction the car was traveling, and saw the street

flowing away before him, with automobiles pressing
on in the foam of the wake, with thick lines of swim-
mers left and right in the mist and the waves. I visited
him once when he was still living in the house on the
knoll on the bank, when, as you recall, there used to
be foliage, fishermen's houses, barns and stables on
the hills, with farms and pasturelands, also a wood.
At that time smallholders lived over there, had goats,
chickens, pigs, and as children we often went over
there Sundays on the ferry and cut ourselves rods from
the hazel bushes, while our parents, mother with her
parasol, father with his bamboo cane, walked along
the paths through the fields. Although the bank over
there belonged to the city, we were out in the country,
hay-wagons came from the fields and cows grazed in
a meadow, slowly coming this way side by side, always
turned in the direction of sunset, of an evening lining
up in a common movement, parallel to one another. I
thought to myself about it, why they always kept the
same direction, and I concluded that it was governed
by a natural economy, whereby they grazed the whole
breadth of the field in a row, missing not a single tuft,
and when they had reached the outermost edge of the
field the grass behind them had grown up again, and
the ferryman, who owned the cows, drove them back
to a fresh start, which for the cows was only a continu-
ation of the same. They chewed the grass into themselves with rolling mouths, meanwhile staring straight
ahead with their dark eyes, made their tails hit their

flanks, from time to time lifted their tails stiffly, broadly braced out their legs, and let steaming, golden-colored water stream out of them, let spicy brown excrements plop down in broad flaps, chewed, lay down, chewed some more, got up again, bent their heads deep into the grass, seized it with their tongues, ripped it off, shoved it into their mouths, chewed and transformed the green brew into white milk, which the ferryman's wife milked from their udders, while the cows stood still, chewing, their heads lifted, staring off over the water, sometimes bawling deep out of their throats. During this procedure we looked on and perhaps she let us take hold the teats and press out a stream, I do not clearly remember, it is so long ago. In any case we followed her, a couple of children from the city, into the house, we carried the pail for her and in the kitchen were allowed to drink out of wooden beakers which she dipped into the pail. The rim of the beaker felt thick on the lower lip and the milk came warm and fat into the mouth and the taste of grass. On the wall hung a white clock, with large ornamented numbers and hands, with a pendulum swinging this way and that and two chains with weights in the form of pine cones. The ferryman sat at the table and had spread out a newspaper in front of him, he read half aloud and sucked on his pipe. His wife looked at us, how we were drinking the milk, and wiped her hands on her apron. The ferryman paid no attention to us and when he saw us on the ferry he pretended not to recognize us how-

ever much we asked him how his cows were and about
the cement dwarf standing in his garden.

My father goes into that white house there, the one
that takes up the whole side of the street. I saw him
clearly, it was my father, I can show you a picture of
him. You can see him here in the photo, the picture
goes back to his early years, he has changed very little,
still has his smoothly parted hair, still wears this tight-
fitting suit with sloping shoulders, these pointed, light-
yellow shoes with gray spats. Perhaps he is still living
in this house, or has his business here. A huge building, the outside wall covered with slabs of white stone,
down below the reception hall and salesrooms, over
the rows of offices, yet no sound from the typewriters and adding machines comes through the walls and
double windows. From the staircase of the uppermost
story he opens the door of his apartment, a sound recognized by the children out back in their rooms, they
hear him clearing his throat, they hear the door closing shut. It is dark in the vestibule, only place where a
little light comes through is the glass door to the corridor. Umbrella stands beside the mirror, on the mirror
dragons or angels, a low table with a silver salver and
in the shadow of the wall the row of things hung up,
everything likely to form youthful memories. Behind
the glass door a long corridor, somewhere on a ramifi-
cation of it my room, a long narrow room with a target
for darts on the door. Stood there in the back part of

the room and threw darts into the round cork plate, with red and blue circles painted on it, and the door opened once when I had forgotten to bolt it and the dart had already been thrown and hit my father in the middle of the forehead, stuck there, with its red tail-feathers, in the white forehead, and he still holding fast to the doorknob.

It is a new house, here before were located the port authority buildings, red brick ones with arched gates leading to courtyards, gates on which flags were hung on holidays on slanting flagstaffs. On the outer quay the tracks for the big traveling cranes are still to be seen, and where dark asphalt border-strips have been laid into the pavement once ran the tracks for the freight cars, which were pulled by the little hissing locomotive with a tapering red breastplate and a bell that rang during the trip and when it was winter smoke hung long in the air in thick white balls. Here stood the warehouses with sliding iron doors, in the warehouse stalls boxes, sacks, barrels were stacked up, here, too, out on the cobbled pavement lay cargo which had been lifted out of the ships, arranged according to category, in its packing, with stamps, numbers, trademarks, names of foreign countries and harbors. What had not been stowed away remained outside at night, roped up and covered with green tarpaulins, and a couple of watchmen walked up and down the sparsely lighted quayside with a revolver holster at their belts, perhaps with a dog, too, which they led on a leash. One of the ferry-man's sons worked here, as a packer, in the winter, in the summer he went to the booths at the fair, there he stood, Jim, his bristly head bent far back, on a platform, surrounded by colorful pictures in which you could see snakes and lions, buffalo and Indians, uniformed apes, palm trees, cannibals and pirate ships. Into his gaping mouth he thrust the broad shining sword, deep into the gullet, down through his throat, into his stomach, until only the pommel was showing and after he had spread his arms out sideways slowly he drew it out again and the spittle and gastric juices dripped from the blade. And when things were in full swing at the docks and more help was needed, Jem could be seen there, too, called in by Jim, and he stuck a steel hook into a crate, swung it to him and with his one hand did more work with draw-chains and nets than many another with two hands. However, farther along ev-erything is still the way it used to be, customs house, shipping offices, freighters, and despite the rolling iron-tired cartwheels, despite the pounding feet, the nets and the chains slid over the ground, despite the rust, the spilled oil and the hot water from the locomo-tive, grass is growing everywhere between the stones, at the base of the warehouses, on the cemented slopes the grass stands high, with stinging nettles and thistles, soon the grass will overgrow the quay, the stones will be broken to bits sprung apart by the grass, bushes will grow out of building walls, roots will take hold in every joint, cracks will split open in the walls and everywhere seeds blown in by the wind will, consuming themselves, get a fasthold in the sand-dust, a wilderness will arise from the rubble and years later we shall crawl about here through the undergrowth, discover remains of buildings, rusted tracks among roots and mosses, and within the ruins everything will be thickly hung with spider webs, even now the spiders are at work, spinning spinning, in the corners of the warehouses, over there the window openings with iron bars on them are full of thick gray webs which swing in the draft, the panes broken, grass in the loam-dust in the cracks of the window frames, in the bird droppings, flocks of birds will nest here, wild dogs, wild cats will roam through the bushes.

At night everything here is forsaken, not even a watchman to be seen. On such a night I carried something down here, from the old city, I came running along the alleyway bent forward, puffing, because what I was carrying was the essence of seven years of prejudice, habit and fallacy, which had suddenly fallen into my lap, I had it all, every bit to myself, could no longer share it out and shove it off onto someone else, nor could I throw it away, either, for it was still my property, it still belonged to my seven fat years, and I lugged it here down the steep alleyway, down to the quay, on the double, and for the occasion I came up with all sorts of art things, so as to get away from stuff that for a moment had struck me as meaningful, I let out cries of negation and struck out with my fist, I breathed out steam and let salty water stream out of me, each step was a trampling, each arm movement an annihilation of doubts of wonderful forcefulness, in that my knuckles became bloody because of it, and no one here crossed my path, it was all emptiness among the formless heaps in their packing, the crates, the trestles and hawsers, untrammeled I could rage about with my property, tinkling and with pointed red breast, until, hours later, I climbed up the alley again, past the monument up there, the eagle with the outspread wings, a hare in his claws, opened the house gate through which I had left, climbed up the stairs, five stories, a steep spiral in crudely slapped-together walls, a stone shell all spotty and scraped away to nothing, holes bored into the plaster by poking fingers made bigger, at the stair-edges a painted white ornamentation worn out by use and washing, and arrived at the door at the top of the stairs. I could still take it, I could still carry a load and with it rush about at great speed, so much I had proved to myself, and now I stood still, below the stair-landing, leaned against the curve of the wall, the right foot two steps below the left foot, and before me saw the light-blue door, with a slot for letters, a brass doorbell, the kind turned with a winged key, a dark-blue nameplate with white letters. I took in these details so exactly because in each of them I was still recognizing the past I longed for, I stood still, listened hard, was aware of a seething stillness, in it a splashing and dripping. Behind the door, the key to which I still carried in my pocket, I heard nothing, and now I imagined as in setting a stage the objects and spaces behind the door, the doormat, and on along the runner, on to the walls with the burlap pasted on them, walls on which hung pictures of bulls, suns, lightnings and fire-spewing mountains, past the clothes-hangers with pieces of clothing, her fluffy overcoat, her raincoat, her kerchief, her checkered sports cap, the boots under it, as far as the door leading to the adjoining room. I cross the big room quickly, it was dark by now, she lay behind in the bedroom, under the sloping window, through which on a clear night the moon and the famous constellations were to be seen. And now he was looking out with her from the bed through the high window, or he twisted himself and looked at her, saw the strands of black hair spread out on the pillow, saw her mouth, her nipples outlined blackly on the fair skin. In the mirror on the back wall lay pooled the inverse image of the big anteroom, in which the recessed windows in the wall stood flung open, and through them came the same sounds from the street that I heard in muffled version from my vantage point. By the apartment door on the landing was a box that once had served for storing firewood, it was long empty now, I lifted the cover and crept into the box, inside which there was a smell of moldering bark. And I still carried everything with me into the box, my arms full of riches, and nested myself down in the wood-dust, lay there awake until it became lighter, then climbed out again, again took up my post in the winding stairs, leaning on a pilaster, left foot two steps below the right foot, ready with a nimble turn to resume my course about the arena. Coming up from the streets could be heard the sounds of milk bottles rattling and the banging of garbage pails being emptied into garbage trucks, and down below in the stairwell doors opened and slammed shut, and children skipped down the steps on the way to school. Steps hesitantly approached, came to a halt here and there, followed by the sound of mail slots opening and falling shut, whereupon slowly I went down the stairs and as he with the mailbag came by I looked the other way and tied my shoelace. Up above he threw a letter into the slot then, breathing heavily, descended, throwing himself from step to step, a heavy older man, and now I looked him in the eye, we recognized each other, he went past, smelling of sour leather, fell step by step into the depths, and soundlessly I climbed up again, and stood just below the landing and heard how the letter was being picked up within, heard her voice and his voice, then through the ventilator in the wall next to the door I heard how she lit the gas stove, put coffee on, set cups out on the table and over it all lay seething silence. Over there the man in the black suit, with the stiff black hat and the black sun-glasses, he could be the one I had seen her with coming out of the house that time, he was dressed differently then, wore brown Manchester pants, a brightly check-ered shirt, a checked cap. I stood concealed in the en-trance arch across the way from them in order to avail myself of the drama of it, as they went close by me arm in arm, and I followed them, waited behind the eagle statue, and when they had gone up and away I sneaked after them, I showed how tenacious I was, I don't know how many days and nights, no end of it in sight, it had been merely a beginning, I had hardly dared face up to the first scene of the play. There I stood, before I ended up that time in quayside precincts, having pressed for-ward into the middle of the room upon returning from a journey, having already seen his topcoat, his jacket outside in the clothes closet, and heard his voice, which grew louder when I went in, and now I saw him, com-fortably leaned back on the low sofa in shirtsleeves, barefoot, and she on a cushion on the floor in front of him, her arms on his knees, her face turned toward me, white as the walls of the room, and in this second the plunge downward began, I fell and fell, and the room, the house, everything fell with me until the stage of weightlessness had been reached, whereupon I flew this way and that, out and away and down, in a single swoop down five stories, along the street, to the beauti-ful hard flat surfaces and sharp-edged posts, amid which everything was fixed and steady and could rever-berate on me, and then again up and into the box and mornings before the gas flame, the clinking of coffee cups, the wordless voices and down into hiding in the gateways and courtyards, up there between those baked-together walls, there where the street runs into the square and the green feathers of the bird materialize, the bird that is perhaps no eagle at all but a parrot, and there where I crept up the stairs to skulk at the threshold. So it was, as countless times before I come up the familiar staircase, dressed in black after my father's funeral, hold the key ready in my hand and hear, before I stick it into the keyhole, voices and sounds from within which create the impression that I am in a strange domicile. Hesitantly I open the door, again I recognize the clothes closet, but the articles of clothing in it are strange to me, no traces of my earlier presence are to be discovered. The laughter of the woman within dies away, by the same token the man's laughter becomes all the louder, and I walked from the entrance hall into the living room in which I have lived for years, but which now harbors strangers. The eyes which greet me stare at me as if I were an intruder, carried by momentum I advance to the middle of the room, still bent on taking possession of it, on lying down there on the low red sofa, on taking off my shoes, stretching out after the journey, for the woman still seems familiar to me, her face, her hair, her morning coat I have often seen, but already I am beginning to wonder, perhaps it's her sister, a distant relative, someone only remotely like her, besides her face before had more color, now it melts into the whiteness of the wall, the features no longer are recognizable, and I raise my finger, want to say something, explain my presence, but I cannot get the words out. On the other hand the man speaks right up to the unbidden guest, he takes the glass standing on the table by the flask and drinks to me, the woman draws nearer to the sofa and holds fast to the recumbent man's naked foot. And while the strength which has been impelling me forward suddenly reverses itself and with a rapidity that steadily increases pulls me downward, I still stand balanced on the flatness of the floor and thus press the flying floor with me into the depths, I am forced to recognize that my visit has been a mistake, that perhaps I did indeed live here once, that perhaps, too, the period of seven years which floats before me has a certain validity, but that thereafter, however, intervals followed which I lost out of sight and reckoning and despite a dim and distant remembrance renewed, nothing any longer fits in with my old ideas. At this moment I wanted to prevail over time become unrecognizable, I continued to keep my forefinger upraised in order to explain this lost time away as a nullity, yet in the swiftness of my downward plunge any movement backward was impossible, it was only evident that what lay behind me could never be reached again, that nothing was known of me any longer in this room, and the man still nodded at me, glass at his mouth, and the woman's snowy face completely disintegrated.

Once I went through a city, a wandering that lasted for several days and nights. I had stepped out of a bus after the conductor had asked me several times what my destination was and finally, after I could not name it, he had kicked me out. I came through districts where there were docks and shipyards, and when, at a crossing, I ran into the same policeman who had seen me before, he stopped me and asked for my papers. I had them with me, also knew who I was, although that meant nothing to me. As yet I had not forgotten my own name, though I had forgotten what I was doing here and what city it was that I was in. Since my papers were in order I was allowed to go my way. I spent the first night in a room over a bar, the floor sloped sharply, everything was tipped, in bed I first lay with my head toward the foot, then changed my position, and until morning grayed I heard the banging and bawling from below. A washbasin stood on a three-legged stool, the door of the little closet in the corner was wedged shut with a piece of folded newspaper, a bulb with a green glass shade hung down from the ceiling, and beyond the window between fireproof walls a section of a river could be seen, now and then a tug, a launch. The room had an extraordinary immediacy and tangibility, in the morning I knew every bit of grain in the worn wooden floorboards, every bit of the flowered wallpaper, with its grease spots, fingerprints, nails and torn places, it was as if I had spent a lifetime here. On the evening of the next day a couple of large figures walked close by me, right and left, I only felt them, did not see them. Where I spent the second night I do not know, perhaps I slept somewhere on the steps of a quayside landing, I remember the yellow water below me, and an iron ring against which I leaned, and the clatter of a motorboat going by. Not until the evening of the third day had my name completely vanished from memory, I took out my papers, read the personal details inscribed on them, they meant nothing to me. When I got tired I lay down where I was, near the water on a smoothly rolled stretch of street, with wet places, splatters of spit, horse droppings. Lay there and was awake, felt fine, yet far away, saw myself from a distance lying there, did not budge. A couple of men came along and bent over me, their hands were blackened with oil, they wore dark-blue overalls, blue peaked caps with a shipping company badge. When they said they had a good mind to throw me into the water I did not stir, I knew they were testing me. They lifted me up, carried me to the edge of the quay, swung me about a few times and I let it all happen to me. Then they laid me down very close to the edge of the wall and went away. When I turned my face sideways I saw the water against the squared stone blocks, with refuse that had floated there, bits of wood, tin cans, sodden paper, a shoe without a sole, orange peels, foam.

Our footsteps grind in the gravel. A thickly populated city, with stony towers among the trees. The inhabitants here are prostrate, obliterated, soon even the nameplates on their houses will no longer be decipherable. Fresh wreaths, a new stone, still damp at its base. During her last hours I sat by my mother in her bed, in a room painted with shiny white enamel, and at the other side sat my father. She could no longer talk, she showed me what she wanted on a little pad. She indicated to us that we were to put our arms about her shoulders and then she leaned on us and it eased her breathing. She pointed to the pad, I handed it to her, and she wrote it would be nice now to have a cup of coffee. I rang, the servant appeared, we got the coffee. All her life my mother had cleaned other people's apartments and washed their laundry, an old servant's wish for a cup of coffee was a wish for the Sunday day of rest. She had scolded me, she had hit me, years on end, she had punished me with a belt, and she had screamed when my father had come home drunk and my father had beaten me until one day I threw him against the fireplace and the fireplace, with its white tiles, had collapsed, smoking, and Sundays we had drunk coffee in the kitchen. When she had emptied her cup I saw that she was holding my father's hand, they were both staring into space, my father and my mother, holding each other's hand, and my arm lay about their shoulders and we were the model of a family. She asked for her writing materials and wrote something with a shaky hand that I was able to spell out only later on. Then she became restless, scarcely had we helped her to get up out of bed than she let go her waters. I led her to the bed, looked for the pot, but did not know how I was to set her on it, and doing all this to me it was as if she were going to bear a child, as if it were her amniotic fluid that was warmly streaming over me, and so she died, lying backward over the edge of the bed, her legs spraddled out wide.

Here they lie in layers, among fish fossils, giant horse-tails, ammonites, saurian bones and tin toys. Our steps crunch in the gravel of the paths. The ferryman once said to me, you can never really know who your father is and who is the father of your son. He told me about Jym. In later years this fellow had begun to wash him-self, have his hair cut short, it was still long, but not so long that it hung matted over his shoulders, and his clothes were still far from conservative, he wore nar-row trousers with black-and-white stripes, red silk vests, violet or blue jackets, shirts trimmed with lace. How he had managed to become rich remains a mys-tery, in any case he soon withdrew to a country house at the edge of the city, had servants and two cars, a mistress with blond corkscrew curls and a sunken mouth, and besides these a gardener, a saddle-horse, a groom and a yacht, which was tied up at a landing at the lower boundary of the lakeside property. Many a time at night the ferryman came with his skiff through a canal to the lake, lay there in the darkness and saw how the windows in the big house were festively lit, how the headlights of arriving cars swept through the park, how the guests went up the stairs to the open glass doors, and heard the music and the laughter.

Once, in the summertime, a party of guests came running down to the shore, many threw off their clothes, others jumped into the water with their clothes on, and some of them swam out, one of them coming toward him. The ferryman sat still in his boat and saw how the head in the water was drawing nearer, with the mouth making soft blowing sounds. The swimmer came up to the side of the boat, the ferryman already could see the whites of his eyes shining, and the swimmer's hands stretched out, and the body came after them, and Jym was standing in the boat, bolt upright, naked, dripping. He stood there for some seconds, or minutes, the ferryman did not tell me just how long, then he again dived into the water, headfirst, swam back to the shore.

And when I hear our footsteps in the gravel of the walks, here in this stillness behind the walls, then the other thing comes back to me, the thing that never had an end, and there I am, still lying in the sand, in front of an open barn, and am able to creep for a way along barbed wire, in a narrowly enclosed place overgrown with trees. There is no getting out when I am there, I can forget it all only for a time, by telling myself that I am awake, I am still alive, but then it comes back again, then it is all as before, and I torture myself with thinking about how it is going to happen, with the rope, the ax or by shooting, and again I crawl along the barbed-wire entanglement, and then back to the barn, and then I debate with myself about how I still might be able to escape, I imagine a feigned suicide, in which I cut the arteries in my wrist, smear myself with blood, and then I see them coming, perhaps they bury me on the spot, but perhaps they might tickle me and then I would have to laugh and I would be given the coup de grace. And if I am buried alive how shall I get out of the ground, many hundredweight of earth over me, my mouth full of earth. I could climb up a tree and then get away by swinging from tree to tree, but they are standing under every tree, they are laughing already, sooner or later I shall fall down into their arms. The trees are there to camouflage this area, there is a thick square of them and outside lies open field. I hear our steps in the gravel, I am awake, I think of the field, it lies clearly before me, I see each blade of grass on it, each flower, with the humming insects, I smell the earthy smell, I must have reached this field at some time or other, otherwise how could I see it so clearly, how could I, otherwise, be walking among you, how could I hear this gravel crunching if I were still lying there on the sand in front of the barn, at the barbed-wire barrier. Or do they have me already in their rifle-sights, are they letting me thrash about for a joke, and then I forget it all again for a time, thinking of this field right here and this gravel walk.

There they come, beyond the double gate, in their black, smoothly polished conveyance, they wear top hats, they sit up stiff and straight, they are hung with gold and silver, the driver glued to the steering wheel, the escort on ahead on motorcycles, in shiny black leather, and the onlookers stand pressed close together at the curbs. Now they come to a stop before the double gates. They get out, small, corpulent people with the fat force-fed faces of babies, the two smallest carrying a wreath behind which they all but disappear from view, they lay it down before the bowl at the gate, the bowl in which the eternal light burns, they take off their top hats, and the ones wearing uniforms salute with their hands at the peaks of their caps, and the women hold their hands folded on their stomachs, and the children gape open-mouthed, and now one of the little ones in front of the place where the light is burning begins to speak, he works his mouth yet his words cannot be heard. He pulls down his mouth with its thick pouty lips, his fat little cheeks begin to quiver, his eyes squeeze together, the veins in his neck swell. And all stare at the little flame, the little flame is reflected in the pupils of all eyes. What is he talking about with words that are not to be heard, he is talking about a game of skat at the regulars' table in the barroom or about the catch of fish last weekend, he is talking about the new suit he has ordered at the tailor's or about his son's bad school report, he is talking about his wife's false teeth or about the lamp that stands on his desk, he is talking about his daughter's illegitimate child, about the sausages he wanted for supper or about the weather that is beautiful today. It is not to be divined, what he says, and again he puts the tall hat on his round infant skull and the others do the same as he, and the hands fall away from the cap peaks, and everyone does aboutface and goes back to the waiting vehicles, the doors of which the drivers are holding open. What are the bystanders screaming, what are they shouting about, why are they throwing their hats in the air. The little fat ones pay no heed, they climb up onto their cushions, the leathery soldiers sit on their bikes in a knightly way, there is a rattle and roaring, then they drive away, leaving the onlookers in a cloud of blue gas.

The littlest one there, in the last car, is Jam, I recognize him now by his description, even though he has lost his red hair, but the gapy mouth, the holes in the puggy nose, the fat fingers are the same. The ferryman told me that he is in the civil service and has gone far, even back in school he was always the best, by squealing on his classmates to the teacher and no one dared beat him up because the teacher was on his side. Although they all hated him, most of them did his bidding, did his homework for him, carried his books for him, just so he would put a good word in for them. One of them who made no bones about being against him was kicked out of the school, for according to the story Jam caught him masturbating in the toilets and to prove it was able to point out the runny splotch on the wall. Later he destroyed others, too, by denouncing them as thieves or arsonists, and a teacher unwise enough to question his information, who indeed said out loud in the middle of a lecture that Jam didn't even know the rudiments of the subject matter, was dismissed from his post when Jam caught him making copulatory movements against one of the students. He also came out of the university with highest honors, after his informers had done his written work for him and he had been excused from the oral examinations, though not before the only dean who couldn't be bribed was laid low with a sudden stomach ailment. His uncontested rise took him to high posts, I believe to the position of director of education and head of all existing institutions of learning and culture, he served as model for many busts and medallions and his name was spoken with reverence.

And I know the little one who got into the first car, the one with the little silver stars and the cords on the peak of his cap, he was at the time when I stood before him still of lower rank, if well on the way to being promoted. We stood before him in a long row, our clothes we had removed outside in the corridor, and left on a wooden bench, we stood naked one behind the other, looking at the pimples and fleabites on the back of the man ahead, smelling the stink of sweaty feet and of armpit dampness, slowly we moved forward and the one in the lead was tapped, sounded, questioned, measured, weighed and shoved to one side. What is that, he

asked me when it was my turn and pointed to the scar
and the welt at my ribs in the region of the heart. A
pistol shot, I said. He was sitting behind a writing table
with a copyist at either side and they gnawed on their
penholders, he still held his forefinger outstretched,
then lifted it, bore into his nose-hole, turned it, drew
it out again, wiped his nose with the back of his hand
and stood up. He went around the table and stepped
in front of me. He bent down to my scar and looked at
it from as close as he could get. He touched it here and
there with his forefinger, which was still damp from
nasal mucus, and said the bullet was still in there to see,
which I already knew. I know it is, I said. He looked at
me from under his brows. His moustache, white today,
at that time was still black, and he had bushy black eyebrows. I represent the army, he said. I know you do, I
said. He thought of something to say, it was plain that
he had made a false start and did not know where to
go from there. Then his face suddenly lit up and he
asked what battle it was I had got the slug. In the battle
against myself, I said, I shot myself in the ribs. He sent
an orderly to get a second-in-command to take over so
he could deal with me undisturbed. He led me, naked
as I was, across a courtyard where the women cooks
of the establishment were doing calisthenics, and into
a big room where a table was set for a banquet. All
around on the walls hung coats-of-arms and crossed
flags, and at the end of the hall rose a podium with a
lectern. He ordered me to pull back the chairs from the

table and arrange them in a serpentine row. Then, on hands and elbows, I was to creep in between the chairs as fast as I could, down the line, back and then down again. When I toppled over he struck me with the flat of his hand on my behind and cried up, up, get going, get going, and I hurried on, until I fell again. Then he ordered me to place the chairs at greater distances apart, and I had to jump from one chair to the next, from one end of the hall to the other and then back. Meanwhile figures in uniforms with trimmings in silver and gold had come in through side doors and were watching my exercises. Finally I had to put the chairs back and afterward go up on the podium. The figures sat down at the tables and the leader of the production stood beside the lectern, since he would have disappeared had he stood behind it. Gentlemen, he called out, and his voice was surprisingly powerful, with an expressive force that carried one away. All faces turned expectantly toward us, Gentlemen, you see before you an exemplary defender of our ideals. He tapped with the seal ring on his finger on the protuberance of flesh where the bullet had gone into my ribs, the while continuing his speech. The clinking that you hear, gentlemen, is a pistol slug which the same here shot into his chest with the intention of escaping from the service that confronts him. Subjected, however, to a certain calisthenics assignment, he showed abilities satisfying our strictest standards. Under my leadership he conquered himself. In spite of the bullet in his chest, with which he had wanted to put himself out of the way, he carried out what was asked of him, with glowing zeal he let himself be convinced that for him henceforth there was no evasion. Thus you see, gentlemen, a hero in the former coward and traitor, who will let himself willingly be detailed to the foremost ranks, and there every bit of courage, of endurance, of self-sacrifice, I have forgotten the rest of the speech. Thereafter I lived for years in hiding, in the woods, in sandpits, in an abandoned mine, earned my keep as a day laborer on remote farmsteads, always in flight from the police, until I found a ship where I was allowed to go aboard without papers and thus carried to other parts of the world. What do they amount to, these decades, I am now walking again along the same old streets, every stone, every tree known to me, there lies the exercise yard across which I was driven, the sentry boxes are still standing at the portals of the buildings, freshly painted but still shabby-looking, and the cannon to right and left still stick out their ridiculous barrels at us.

How quickly the mechanized column with its armored van- and rear-guard vanished in the flow of the street, and the people on the sidewalks still stare into the traffic long since closed in again, they are still hearing the sirens, the whistles that announced something was happening, but not a face behind the mirroring panes of glass rushing by had been recognizable. There they go now on their way, walk in through doors, come out through doors, alone, by twos, in groups, already we are coming again to streets earlier traversed, the city is not so big that we could lose our way in it, we always find the way again, it is almost as if we belonged to this forward movement, as if we were at home here, as if we ourselves had come here out of some hole or other, as if there were someone here who was waiting for us.

Here I had my hiding place, in the riverside district, here I lay rolled together, smelled the dampness of the ground, smelled the dampness in the air, under a pile of boards I had made myself at home, and through the cracks I saw the trains on the railroad embankment, I saw how the tugboats tipped down their funnels when they went under the railroad bridge, how the smoke poured out blackly, how the travelers leaned out of the windows and on the way out looked back toward the city and coming in the faces turned away from the city, and I saw the children on the up-sloping scorched meadows, how they let their paper dragons with long gaily colored tails climb into the haze. From my scrap heap, my hole in the ground, where I also lay out straight, I saw the insulators blooming on the high-tension lines, the traffic signals at crossing points in suburban streets, I saw the carts and the trucks which came back in the gray of morning empty from the market hall, and the heavy long-distance trucks with tied-down loads, with the drivers high up on the driver's seat, the furniture vans painted with winged horses, or with the emblems of far-off cities, the cars that came in of a morning, at first one at a time, hastily, an open ribbon of highway in front of them, then ever more densely, sticking stubbornly to each other, slowly moving forward under the electric wires, I saw how the milkshops and the bakeshops opened their doors, how the women bent out of the windows and waved with their dust cloths, I saw the children with school-bags under their arms running to school, I heard the ringing of the bell at the beginning of classes and the pneumatic drills of the street-builders and the crashing of iron plates at the shipyard, I heard the sirens of incoming and outgoing ships from the harbor, and the buzzing of planes muffled by clouds or standing out clearly in blue sky, I heard hammer blows from the allotment gardens where a gardener was fixing his fence, and from the woodworking shop I heard the scream of the circular saw, I saw the garbage truck coming, saw it lower its rump over the dumping spot and empty its wet rushing contents, I saw the dump-pickers rummaging around in the rubbish and I saw couples with their arms linked on the way to the riverbank or to the gravel piles, I saw how they stood still, I saw the changing of the light over the fields, the shacks, the factories, over the height with the newly built houses I saw rain and hail fall, saw the vapor rising out of the ground, heard the striking of hours from tower clocks.

On my travels I once lived on a beach. From my window, or from the sand where I lay, I could see a narrow lagoon, on which trees grew, they looked like palms, but were not palms at all. Nor were there crocodiles and flamingoes, only frogs and swarms of sandfleas. When my skin itched I went into the still water and bathed. Once a week the ship came to the jetty, tied up, then traveled farther along to the next inhabited place, a day's journey away. Often I went aboard, bought provisions and then again went to live on my beach, disturbed by no one. I lived here and did nothing that left a mark behind. At the most the minimum effort serving to keep me fed had any point, catching a fish, picking mushrooms and berries in the woods, or lighting the fire for cooking. Otherwise my thoughts were concerned with nothing in particular, they posed no questions, constructed no answers to fictitious problems. I slept when I was tired, I got up when I had slept long enough. I picked up stones, felt them out, let them fall again. I poked my finger into the sand, drew it out again, I chewed on a splinter of wood, or on a leaf and spat it out again. I saw a bird fly in the air and disappear behind trees, I saw clouds come in and sometimes ball together into thunderheads, I saw clear sky return again. No, it was on an island, I lived the summer there with a numerous family, and I waited for the day when the wife and child, brothers-in-law and sisters-in-law, nephews, female cousins and parents-in-law went back to the city and I could go to work in peace on the work for which I had been collecting material for years while we were moving from one apartment to another, the last always smaller than the one before. So the cutter left, fully loaded, when the vacation period was at an end, I heard the engine die away on the wind that had sprung up toward evening, and I climbed the hill to the log hut. I have often tried to explain to myself what it was that happened that night, and why I did not find the peace and composure I had anticipated, but fled in confusion from the island. The signs of a gathering storm were already unmistakable, the waves rolled in with white foam-crests, the clouds drove along low and broken in the sky, the trees swayed, all natural manifestations, and yet in it all a strange transformation could be felt. It still seemed possible to attain seclusion, to light the oil lamp on the table, get to work on the notes, yet every step I took toward a beginning led me farther from it, the papers lay ready, the lights were lit in all the rooms, but disturbances steadily increased. I stood in the middle of a flash-flood of movements and sounds, I heard each component part of this machinery, made up of water and foliage, boughs and grasses, of posts, bricks, wires and boards, I was able to discover holes and cracks in which the drafts of air got trapped, I heard this whimpering, whistling and hissing, this spraying, rattling, growling, scraping, scratching, squeaking and humming, this explosion of whistling and sucking, I went back and forth in the rooms and identified the origin of each sound until the agitation became so great that everything in it was indistinguishable, and when it made no difference how intensely I listened the other thing began, a quite different rushing and tearing, as if it might be something evoked by the air masses, a banging and rattling not created by the wind, a rumbling not caused by waves on the cliffs, a chattering and singing not possible among leaves and grasses. Now no more thoughts about work. Nights past when I had stepped over beds and gone out in front of the house I had been able to see the relationships among the aggregate of particulars, right off I drew logical inferences, now I had forgotten why it was that I had stayed on here, and all that was left was this pressure, this senselessness, and in this condition I landed outdoors again, perhaps because inside the house I felt myself caught in a trap, I had taken off my clothes, I stood outdoors in the seething rain and bellowed and flailed about with my arms, and ducked under the gigantic lashings of the trees, and this kept up the whole night long until finally, at the first shimmer of dawn, it died down and all that was left was a washed-outness, a feeling of physical exhaustion. What had happened already had become incomprehensible, only something of it had survived, and there were the trees and they stirred in the light spring wind and the grass whistled and the sea breathed in soft swells, and mechanically I packed my trunk, stowed away the papers, turned out the lamps, locked the house and went down to the rowboat lying on the pebbly shore. Going over to the mainland to the place where the steamers came in, all of it took place amid lassitude and a hollowed-out feeling like the feeling after a fever has passed, it was still hours before the steamer was to arrive, yet I was done with the island, I knew no more about the island and the time I had spent there, I tied up the boat, sat on the planks of the bridge in a stillness and emptiness, a uniform breathing, the sun rose in the sky, it became warm, over there the island flickered in the light, with the house on the hill among peaceful trees, and I sat in half-sleep leaned against a pile, and when the steamer whistle sounded from afar it was a signal of victory, and then the ship came up triumphantly, whitely shining, broad-breasted, snorting.

The time that the woman whose name I had forgotten came up to me one afternoon and held up her pregnant belly to me, I was living with someone else, and to this other one I returned after the proceedings in front of the wooden rail in the wooden city hall chamber had been completed. Within an hour I had left her, the one to whom I had sworn eternal fidelity, and who now went her way to bear my child, and I went back to the room where I had left the other one behind, and she sat in the same position in the armchair at the open window which she had taken upon my departure. The floor at her feet was wet from a shower of rain, her legs were wrapped in a blanket, her upper body was covered by a woolen jacket, her hands lay frozen on her knees, her head lay in the pillows, her eyes closed. When I stroked her hands her gaze flickered this way and that for a time before focusing on me. Her pupils were distended, she still did not recognize me, her eyes, the dark-red oval of the iris, the thick violet lashes, stared at me and now and again rolled up so high that only the bluish white eyeball could be seen. When I lowered myself onto her and touched her, shudders of cold passed over her skin, her body rose and sank back, and when she let me into her holding herself open for me with her hands, her face was twisted out of shape with horror. She screamed and clung hard to me, and then lay weeping and nights she awakened me, she sat upright in bed with muscles tensed and whispered, do you hear it do you hear it. What is it, I don't hear anything. How it's cracking and crunching. There in the middle of the room, there's someone cracking nuts and grinding his teeth. There's no one there, I said, and held her tightly. I'm lying on a white balcony, with a thin railing, she cried, and I said that it was an airy balcony and that I could see her from the open door and that it was light and that the balcony was securely fastened to the wall, yet she screamed that the white shutters in front of the balcony door were closed, that the balcony floor was thin as a piece of paper and that she dared not move, that she had to hold her breath so as not to tear the paper. The floor will hold you, I said, yet her face was distorted, her mouth gaped wide open, and then she saw a street, it was a bare street in a clean little city, at the beginning when she told me about this city everything seemed to be quiet and Sunday-like, the pavement was washed, the steps leading up to the

doors shone with cleanliness, yet right away she began to tremble, she was alone in this street, in a short
dress, a basket on her arm, and she began to run and
to scream, why are you screaming, what are you really
afraid of, and I could see nothing but the bare cobble-
stones, the gleaming steps and polished doorknobs,
and she saw only her feet in white buckled shoes flee-
ing down the street. Her child shared this same terror
and with him the terror was even more extravagant
and his shrieking not to be appeased. We lived at the
seashore, had arrived at the outskirts of the settlement
as darkness was falling, amid dwarf pines and thorny
bushes lay the little wooden houses, still empty and
closed up at this time of the year. We walked against
the sea wind, with the child, the baggage and in the
bungalow it was cold and the beds were damp. The big
suitcase, full of sheets and towels, was thickly soaked
by syrup that had run out of a broken bottle. I hung the
clammy blankets in front of the electric heater and she
carried the weeping child in her arms, she walked back
and forth with the child and rocked it, and I warmed
milk and then came the shrieking. She showed me the
big scar that ran across the child's chest and she said
that the screaming came from the time of birth and
that in this screaming still lay the dread of suffocation
and dying, for the child had nearly suffocated at birth
and that they had cut an abscess out of his chest and
it was because of this that he had to scream, and she
walked about with the child amid the blankets hung

on a line and redly lighted up and rocked it in her arms and sang weepily in concert until the shrieking had worn itself out, then we lay down close together under our overcoats and at dawn we saw a fly sitting on the table, big as a man, it looked at us with eyes big as plates, rotated its mandibles and bit into the wings of an insect that it held in its claws, and the venation of the wings crunched and burst like spun glass. And as always, when she began to tremble at my side, when she screamed and when tears rained from her eyes, I could only say, what's the matter now, there's nothing there, I don't see anything, and then she grabbed hold of me, and in moments of clarity she cried, gray dwarf all covered with dust, gray mouse, sowbug, you're going to die from the dust that's stuck your eyes and mouth together, and then she spread herself open to an imaginary lover and when she let me go into her she was not aware of me, I hung over labyrinths and grottoes, over coral reefs and sponge forests, and lost myself inside her, and then she shoved me away from her, screamed with excitement, and I rescued myself by retreating into my indifference and self-control, I played the superior one, it looked as if I were holding together while she was falling apart, yet it was she who was living, even when she consumed herself doing it, I only sat at the window in an armchair and made my phone calls, and went over to city hall and the child in the belly of a strange woman poked me in the side when I pressed against her to seal our adventitious and immediately forgotten marriage with a kiss, and then again I sat in the armchair, and a cry came from the bed, of help me, they're coming now, they're coming now through the leaves, then I called back, it's nothing, it's nothing, be quiet, no one's there, and when the cry came they're grabbing me now and laughing at me and blowing in my face, I stood up and sat down beside her and put my arm about her and acted as though I could protect her, yet she was far away from me, I saw her not at all. And when she went away from me, not because she had met her great lover, but only because it happened that way, because the weather made for it, because the suitcases had fallen out of the cupboard against her, we quarreled on leaving over a broom, she wanted to take the broom along, I said I had bought the broom for the kitchen and for a while we both held onto the broom and tugged at it, and then she let me have it and I shoved it between my legs and took her bags and went out, and I flew on the broom about the house and experimentally flew for a way out the window, riding on the broom, and I saw her down below in the street, a suitcase in either hand, dressed in a red shawl, slung about her body and held by a cord, in gold-lacquered sandals, her hair falling down over her shoulders. Here, I will show you here an envelope with a black mourning border, here look, a strand of hair, color not recognizable, and here, she and I, arm in arm, a happy couple at the shore of a lake, her child with us, all three laughing, our black shadows behind us. The letter with the black border was received by my father from his father, when he informed him of the death of his wife, my father's mother, my father carried the letter about with him, with his mother's picture and the lock of his mother's hair, and the locks of hair lay in thin tissue paper, they still lie there, perhaps I have taken out the wrong one at times, or have got them mixed up, I have been carrying the letter with me a long time, since my father's death.

There you see Jom, at the entrance to the subway, the fourth ancient son of the ferryman, in rags, on crutches, babbling great sayings. After the household broke up he was driven out and had to start life on his own, it no longer did him any good when he pounded the floor with his stick or banged on the table, no one appeared, no mother any more brought him the pap he could swallow with his toothless mouth, he had to see how he could make out on his own, and he understood nothing. According to what the ferryman said it appeared that Jom lived somewhere among the packing paper and corrugated cardboard in the rubbish pile behind the railroad bridge, and if it is at all possible it must be there that he composes his odes, theme of which is that he knows nothing, that he understands nothing, that he cannot grasp just why he is where he is now or why he is at some other place, why he happens to run into this person or that one, why it is that it gets dark or light, or rains, or hails. If it can be so,

there it is that he practices his hymns, perhaps writes
them down, too, on moldy paper swollen with damp,
out of the ferryman's garbled words I gathered that he,
Jom, could be seen there, in his balled fist a stub of
pencil, a flat, broad pencil thrown away by a carpenter,
and the while he shook his head and spittle ran out
of his mouth over his stubble of beard, he wrote and
wrote but the rain washed it all right away. He, who is
not capable of speech, makes these sounds come out,
they sound like salve, malve, half, laugh, fold, cold,
bold, rolled and so on, the words can be translated as
you will. Still, now when I see him here I am not sure
whether it really is he, rather I believe that the Jom the
ferryman talks about sits today in one of the high-rise
apartments in the suburbs, in an apartment with a high
rental, at a writing table with a glass top, in front of
a bare picture window looking out over playgrounds,
auto factories and bus stops, and knows exactly where
he is sitting and what he is writing down, and soberly
he hammers out letter after letter, word after word on
the typewriter and reads over the sentences, nodding
his head.

Earlier at one time we went over this bridge, which
sways under our feet. Its wood is rotten, it creaks at
the joints, the pontoons are thickly crusted with bird
droppings, the chains are overgrown with mussels and
algae. There the traffic is held up, a horse has fallen in
front of a coach, a roan sprinkled with red, the shafts

are broken, the coachman stands by and curses, the occupants of the coach have gotten out, a bridal couple, her veil flutters, he holds his top hat, too large for him and hired for the occasion, fast on his head. Has a white chrysanthemum in his buttonhole and she carries a bunch of roses and the floor of the bridge sinks under the stalled traffic. Already the sirens and the policemen's whistles are coming and in the cars they sit patiently at the steering wheels, not yet knowing what has happened, will never know, only sit and wait in outpouring blue gas, wait and are everywhere awaited.

These windows, these tables, bookshelves and cabinets under the fluorescent lights, divided up by glass walls, when I look in on this place it seems to me I once went in and out here every day the year round, with great authority vested in me, the porter in his dark green uniform took off his cap to me on the stairs, people passing by bowed, a young lady in a tight jumper held the door open for me, stood ready with her stenographer's notebook when I walked into the room and sat down at the big desk. I laughed at myself, looking out from a richly decorated golden frame, broad-shouldered, rosy, with fillings in my teeth, and whoever else confronted me from the desk top, if not my wife and children, all were laughing and well-fed. No, a cloth hung over the picture on the wall, I could no longer bear to look at it, only during contract signings when the representatives of great organizations were present was the picture unveiled, and when my wife was announced, because she happened to be in town and needed money, for a hat, a tart, was her picture taken out of the drawer and placed on the desk top. I banished my assistant from the room, the hour had not yet come when I would go with her into the small side-room behind the padded door, where a couch stood ready and a table with drinks, it was early in the morning, I wanted to be alone and gird myself for the day. When she had shut the door behind her I threw myself down on the desk, put my head on my arms and sobbed for a quarter of an hour, then I straightened up in the swivel chair, the back of which could tip far back behind me, and thus sat, my hands locked behind my head, feet on the desk, and looked through the window out on the park, through which we are walking right now. Just as now the rooks were flying upward in great flocks, they were the forefathers of the present ones, the remote ancestors, and they scrawked hoarsely as their posterity scrawk today. On such a desk as the one on which my legs lay, in the morning the stack of incoming mail rises up, already taken out of the envelopes and spread out, and I read the heading of the topmost piece of writing, it comes from the Society for the Abolition of World Poverty. This must be an important office, a headquarters in which decisions of great moment are made. By all appearances it had to do with the distribution, lending or collection of money, I can no longer recall exactly, only remember the big figures that were discussed. Still shaken from time to time I leafed through the letters, underscored the sums named and drew little men on a sheet of paper that lay there ready for that purpose. Then I turned a knob on the intercom apparatus on my desk and right off breathing sounds could be heard coming from it, I needed only to whisper and a voice answered, and immediately thereafter she walked in, in her tight jumper, and the day's work could begin. Although both calculations and correspondence had been finished, the real activity consisted of seeking out, discarding and building up mutual relationships, in all the divisions, all this was hard to take in at a glance, seldom was obvious, for the most part lay concealed in operations that had a practical appearance, thus I could walk in anywhere and all I would see by a typewriter were two heads behind large unfolded papers, whereas down below out of sight hands held each other, or I saw the gaze of a person who carefully and regularly kept accounts apparently directed at a table of figures that he was holding up for me to see, whereas actually it was directed at a neck some distance away. Discussions of portfolios meant making rendezvous for the following evening, a hurried wandering together down the corridor had for its purpose not the completion of a series of telegrams but vanishing into a cloakroom. In my padded dictation room few words were lost, hardly was the door closed than she was pulling her jumper over her head and unbuttoning her dress and, after some days or weeks, according to the duration of our mutual accommodation, she carried out the same act of submission in other departments while new assistants made their appearance with me. And meanwhile our comprehensive effort flourished, it bloomed as money came pouring in, and what flowed out was expected as a matter of course to produce a multiple return, we had time for everything while the apparatus was working for us, and from the office boys' waiting room to the marble hall used by management's highest echelon we could all go our secret ways. No, I moved about in these rooms amid unspeakable toil, I walked sideways, my arms full of documents, carried them back and forth from one table to another, punched endless columns of figures into the machines, delivered reports, ran along the corridor to get new assignments, until I got a responsible post with the highest administrator, and for him took care of the purchase of wine-cellars, autos and racehorses, and was helpful to him in negotiations for a medieval fortress, with towers and moats. I had got used to walking sideways and dragged one leg behind me, and many here walked the same way, sideways or backward or bent far forward or taking a hop every third step, according to the kind of task with which they had been charged. If I am not mistaken in many of the rooms the secretaries were bound fast to their chairs, and when they stood up they carried their three-legged stools about with them on their behinds. When I think back on this time I see us all taking part in a tireless common effort, walking bent over, crawling, lying on our bellies between mechanical constructions, and only in the afternoon, in the hour between two and three, did we often sink into breathlessness, into a paralysis out of which only the scrawking of the rooks awakened us. No, it was not like that, I am seeing it wrong, it is so long ago, rather we found ourselves in an adventure, in a hectic game, in a raging tension, mornings we stormed up the stairs, threw ourselves at the mountain of incoming letters and telegrams, ripped the strips of paper out of the teletype which had ticked on throughout the night, and while we got the announcements and offers straightened out, with glowing zeal the loudspeaker system, the phones, the incoming messengers called to us to carry out new commissions, we had to come to our decisions lightning fast and function according to altered circumstance, we were breathless at our work in our main office, green eyeshades over our foreheads, black glasses before our eyes, gliding this way and that in the blinding light, numbers flashing all about us. Coffee, sandwiches were brought in, we had no time to go out to eat, and absence of a few minutes could destroy the work of years, could mean our ruin, until late at night we stuck it out and loaded mounting wealth into the safe. No, it was not like that, either, it was only a great disjointedness, a boundless agitation, in which we all kept watch on one another. I still see myself jumping up on a table, a heap of papers in my arms, and throwing the papers into the air, some of them folded into swallows, others into darts, others crumpled together, paper after paper, and then letter-files out of hard, pressed cardboard with a hole to hold them by the forefinger, they flew crosswise through the hall, some broke apart as they flew, and the leaves came tossing down, piled on top of each other, onto the type-writers and the buckled-down typists, and in a couple of places the glass partitions were smashed, faces appeared in the jagged holes, redly swollen, one running blood, and the typists leaped up with their chairs on their behinds and I jumped from desk to desk, sprang over the screaming typists and out of adjacent rooms the department heads, the assistant and general managers came running and a bunch from the board of directors and honorary chairmen, some of them were pushed in in wheelchairs, a meeting of the principal stockholders had just been held, and an old lady was flailing around with her umbrella, she was said to be the biggest investor, half of all profits belonged to her, her head trembled, she was carried by two general directors and right away one of the portfolios hit her, slung sure of its aim, backward she fell, her legs, in black woolen stockings, kicked about in her petticoats and outside the rooks threw themselves at the window-panes, dashed with yellow beaks against the vibrating glass. Oh no, I sat patiently and unobtrusively at my desk, wearing black protective sleevelets in order to preserve the jacket of my only suit, mornings I came to my duties punctually, and evenings I rode back in a bus, a firmly wedged-in part of the whole, arm in arm, shoulder to shoulder with my own kinds, in the flow of the street.

Here, behind the freight depot, at this spot between high factory buildings, one time I was lying behind the boxwood bushes in the enclosure at the train platform fence. I had landed here after being unable to solve certain problems in connection with wife and child. I don't know how long I tried to find a solution, whether I assumed from the start that finding a solution was out of the question and only pretended it might be possible. In any case I had been preoccupied with the matter for a long time, the child had already learned to talk when I took off this evening. My attempt to solve the problem, or at least my alleged attempt, was involved in almost everything that went on in the apartment. I picked up a plate, my wife asked, why that particular plate. I explained, while holding up the plate between thumb and forefinger, that the plate seemed to be suitable for the purpose I had in mind. For what purpose, she inquired. My answer was, for example, for the purpose of holding the food I had it in mind to cook. What kind of food, my wife asked. Noodles, for instance. Or grits, or beans. To her the plate seemed too small for that. Or, if baked cheese slices, or plum dumplings were in prospect, too large, there was no need to fill it full. She considered this to be superfluous and brought to my attention the fact that the very multiplicity of plates which she had brought as a dowry was to make it possible to have the proper plate at any given time. In a united effort we selected other plates from among the high piles of porcelain with which the cupboard was filled, in the course of which maneuver towers of plates were taken down and had to be put back again one on top of the other, always making sure that the child did not run into the unloaded heaps. I said to my wife, stick to your machine, do your work, I'll do mine, but she said that even I could see how far I was getting with my work. If I said it's better that you finish sewing the nightgowns that have been ordered and leave setting the table to me, she said how much it meant to her that this time we ate from the plates with the checkered blue pattern at the rim and that anyhow she had to sew shirts and blouses far into the night. Also in the cupboard were our towels, tablecloths and sheets, and, since they partly covered the tableware, they had to be taken out of the drawers and, since they would get dirty on the floor, laid out on the bed. I took out a glass. The glasses were packed closely together in the topmost drawer, and in order to choose among them I had to climb up on a chair. We had numerous kinds of glasses, all in all the contents of the cupboard constituted our sole riches, everything else hardly bore mentioning. When I had taken out a glass for myself, a glass for my wife and a third glass suited for the child and had put the glasses on the table, she asked why I had picked out those glasses. I explained to her that in my opinion the form and volumetric capacity of the glasses in question were in line with the drinks that I intended to pour into them for the meal. For example, water, or beer. These glasses, she retorted, were intended for wine. And so again we climbed up, I meanwhile drawing up a second chair, up to the cupboard. Again I placed the glasses I had removed back in the drawer and instead took out the glasses that my wife preferred, while the child crept under the chairs and had his hand trodden on by me stepping down. Taking care of the hand led to numerous differences of opinion. I wanted to wash the hand, my wife found washing injurious in this case. I came up with a band-aid, my wife found that in this case a bandage was better. I bound the hand with the bandage, but it had to be unbound, because I had wound it too tight. Meanwhile the dish that I had in the pot or pan had boiled away or burned up, it was always hard for me to keep to the precise boiling or broiling time, and my wife asked me whether she had to do all the boiling and broiling, too. At this point the discussions were already becoming more involved and could not be settled by a simple for or against, in which my wife's viewpoint finally won the day. I had taken over the cooking, table-setting, dishwashing, cleaning up and childcaring, since my wife was supporting us with her work on the sewing machine. When now and then there was a quarter of an hour during which the child had fallen asleep and no pressing chore lay at hand, I devoted myself to another activity, I sat down

at the table, that is, if the table were clear, and not filled
with pieces of clothing that had to be sewed, and
spread my papers out in front of me, the papers on
which I had written the notes for my scientific work. I
tried to read what I had written down and to remember
what it was I wanted to say with the matter inscribed.
Scarcely was I sitting still, bent over the papers, face
propped on my hand, forehead wrinkled, than my wife
turned to me. She had a thread in her mouth and her
feet kept right on working at the treadle under the machine, she nodded at me and asked how I was getting
along. I could not miss hearing a note of contempt in
her query and I replied, if I had the peace of mind and
the leisure, and she nodded again and said, the thread
between her lips, that in such case we would have the
peace of mind and leisure to starve. Since she was right
I could say nothing to this and the quarter-hour passed
without my grasping the sense of the notes, let alone
writing down anything new. Finally I just sat there,
leaned back, had a look at the ceiling and walls of the
room, our bed, the child's crib, my wife's back, the
pieces of fabric hanging over chairbacks, the round-
breasted torso of the dressmaker's dummy, the cupboard, that great lump of a portable cupboard, which
took up a third of the room, the kitchen nook, the door
to the washroom, the door to the corridor, the window
beyond which all to be seen was a building front with
other windows. When I wasn't writing I still had to take
care of my pipe, I knocked out the ashes, dug the oily

tobacco dottle out of the bowl, twisted off the stem, cleaned the nicotine residue out of it, shoved the pipe together again, filled it, lighted it up, let the smoke come puffing out, while the sewing-machine needle frenziedly pierced the cloth, my wife bent forward, bit off the thread, turned the cloth to a new position and then, having become suspicious because of the quiet at the table, turned toward me, her feet always tramping away at the treadle. She said I was getting everything dirty with my ashes and tobacco leavings. I replied that the by-products of my smoking were going into an ash-tray. She said that my smoking was hurting the child. Complicated trains of thought lay behind her criticism, for she meant not only the smoking, in the smoking she saw only an expression of my idleness, and I tried to explain to her that smoking stimulated my brain, that while I was sitting still I was full of meditation. Yet when she bent at this to her work once more with a snuffing sound from her nose, I had to admit she was right, for the pipe-smoking did not in fact lead to any world-shaking results, all that happened was that I heard the spittle bubbling in the tobacco, my throat hurt from the biting smoke and the ashes, the burnt matches and the sooty, gummy tobacco dottle merely represented so much money thrown away, and I strove to find one small detail in the complicated process that stood in my favor, yet none did I find. I knew before I started that when I sat down at the table I would ac-complish nothing in the short span of time allotted me,

and yet sit down I did, took out my papers, looked up
some inconsequential thing or other. Even when on
one occasion I wrote something down on the paper I
knew that it said nothing, nonetheless I wrote it down,
read it over, nodded and pretended that it meant something to me. For some minutes I threw up a bulwark, I
entrenched myself behind the papers, and the pencil
was my weapon. The pencil point broke, it had to be
sharpened. That took some time. The knife was full
and had to be whetted. The pencil-dust and the shav-
ings had to be cleared away. And then the child woke
up, or I had to run to the market because I had forgotten the onions for the herring. In the evening when the
child had grown quiet with the aid of a soporific, when
the plates had been washed up and put back into the
closet, the pots scoured, the table wiped clean, the
day's expenditures totted up, I might perhaps have had
more time for my writing activity, but it was just now
that most of the customers came, fetched finished sewing jobs, brought new ones, haggled about the price,
tried on blouses, skirts, jackets a number of times, during which business I had to withdraw into the bath-
room. Sitting on the toilet I had my best thoughts,
thoughts which in any event for a while seemed meaningful to me, but when I went into them more closely
they, too, proved to be no good. Later in the evening
when the last customers had gone, my wife naturally
was tired, I myself was not tired, however much taking
care of the house took up my time. I wanted to sit some

more in my chair, but my wife wanted to sleep and the light burning prevented her from doing it. When she took her clothes off I wanted to take hold of her, when I saw her in her slip, or naked, I lusted for her, yet she said, what do you want, what are you grabbing me for. I stroked her flat breasts and thin hips, yet when I pulled her into the bed I had to turn the light out, she wanted to lie in the dark. It took quite a while for my eyes to get used to the subdued shimmer of light that came through the window from the streetlamps. It was hard to tell whether my wife was asleep or awake, she had closed her eyes, did not move, let out not a sound, while I was busy with her. Gradually the objects in the room became distinct, the dressmaker's dummy with its little round head, its broad hips, its erect bosom stood at the foot of the bed and watched my exertions. I got up, took the dummy under the arm and hid her behind the cupboard. It was on such a night, when the collective laughter of a quiz-hodgepodge and the rush of waterfalls was penetrating through the walls that I suddenly sprang out of bed, dressed and ran out, landed in freight-station precincts and there threw myself down behind the boxwood hedge. Years later I learned what she had kept from me. In her eyes I was a criminal, I behaved like a madman in her apartment, hit her, threw silverware at her head, and when her customers had undressed I came leaping out of the toilet where she had sequestered me, so they had to flee screaming into the hall, and while the child howled I threw myself on her, tore off her clothes, tipped over the sewing machine and finally flung myself headfirst out through the window, unfortunately not smashing myself to smithereens in the street.

The ferryman told me once about his wife. He described her differently to me than I remembered her. I saw her as still fleshy, stout, with her hair drawn back in a bun on her neck, with a wart on her nose and I did not recognize the picture he had of her, for he described her as haggard, almost a head taller than he, with red hair, apparently a wig, and he knew nothing about a wart on her nose, on the contrary, he told about a growth of beard unknown to me. He told me how evenings she sat before the door of the house and sang. Without taking his pipe out of his mouth he imitated the tone of this singing, it was like a yowling or the bleating of sheep, and this seemed to be true to the mark, for according to what he said the animals whose voices she was mimicking when she sang slowly came to her from all sides and listened to her, and yowled, meowed and bleated along with her, and while she sang she kept her eyes closed and swayed from side to side. The ferryman, too, went outdoors when this singing was going on, and one or the other of the sons, above all Jom, the oldest, who here learned the rudiments of his later litanies, and because she sang only on beautiful evenings, and not when it was stormy or raining, a yellowish or greenish sky was to be seen, and beyond the river lay the city, with the windows in the houses yellowish or greenish. In winter, when snow lay deep about the house and the animals were in the barn and it was inadvisable on account of the weather to go outdoors, sometimes the wife went into a dance, by the full of the moon, I believe. The ferryman showed me, standing at the steering wheel, his idea of this dance, alternately he raised the right then the left leg to one side, letting the other fall, and I saw that he had tears in his eyes. For now the other wife came to his mind, the other wife into which one day this one had turned. She went to put food for Jym in front of the box, as she did every evening, she went out with the full wooden trough and came in without a trough, as usual, yet now she was small and shriveled, a little dwarf, sharp-nosed, crook-legged, with stringy black hair, red eyes. Who are you. I'm your wife, she said. Weren't you just tall and red-haired. No, I am as I am, am as I am, she replied. She stayed that way. She danced no more and she sang no more, yet other than that she did all her work as before, only more slowly, more helplessly.

That time on the island, during the night I was telling you about, for the first time I saw what leaves are. When I had gone up to the house and was standing in front of the bushes and trees I saw those thousands of leaves, each in a different place fastened to the branch with a thin stalk, and each leaf moved, rose and fell, quivered this way and that, still silvery bright on the

surface, darkly shadowed below, and in the rising wind
the branches lifted, became pressed downward, in a
common rhythm, and the thousands of leaves struck
each other softly, thousands of thin, rattling little
plates, each shot through with veins, with a fine venation running from the middle vein outward, each
arranged according to the same system, and yet each
different from the other, still the flickering light lay on
them, and in their twistings and turnings they reflected
the lightness that broke through the tattered cloud,
and then the trunks began to bend and straighten up
again, and when they went down the leaves, standing
upright on their stems, rushed downward, and when
the trunks rose the leaves rose, bent backward, with
a whistling sound, and this repeated itself constantly,
while the clouds massed ever more thickly together
and shut off the light. For a long time I stood in front
of the house under the spell of the rushing sound, of
the dance of the trees, and as I stood there it was as if
I were stretching myself out, away over the hill and as
far as into the woods, my fear lay spread about in the
grasses, the woodland, the cliffs, was taken up by all the
leaves, and stormed back on me again, with the surf-
foam, the buffets of the storm.

What I said about the ferryman's former house was
wrong. I have never been in the house, I have only
stood at the fence and thought I could see the kitchen
through the window, with the whitewashed super-

structure of the fireplace, I looked between the fence pickets, between the sorrel leaves, and saw how the woman came with the pails from milking. In the barn the calves lowed and the cows called back from the field, there was a lamentation in this calling out, for the calves were not allowed to be with their mothers, they stood held fast by wooden stanchions, immediately after birth they were taken from their mothers, they cried for their mothers' teats and the cows cried out for their young ones' soft muzzles, but only the pummeling hands of the ferryman's wife pulled at their udders, drawing the fat foaming milk out of them into the pail, and the calves got a watery mixture poured into the trough, and over this they yammered and the cows lifted their heads and stared with big uncomprehending eyes out over the city, and let out their own muffled cries. When the ferryman's house was torn down and the excavations began for the new buildings, Jum, the fat one, was left behind on the old property. It is said that he did not want to leave the place of his birth, that no power was great enough to drive him out of bed and out into all the world's winds. In his description of the collapse of the household the ferryman did not mention his wife and the other sons, it is possible at the time he was living alone with his favorite son. Long ago the surveyors had come with their white stakes and had rammed them into the ground, the fence had been knocked down by tractors with caterpillar treads, there were no more cattle nor any barn and the trees lay there with their roots become all cartilaginous. The frame of the building was already going up and the brightly painted kettle of the cement-mixer turned. Ladders were laid against the leany old house, workmen climbed up them, whistling and singing, and lifted the tiles from the roof and, using rammers, hit the walls from the inside so that beams and stones fell in heaps. In the clouds of dust Jum lay there in bed, the eiderdown coverlet drawn up over his ears and in between the trips he had to make down below on the river the ferryman ran up to him, sat by him, held his hand, fed him and talked baby-talk to him. The crumbled stones were carted away and when the floor planking was loosened workmen lifted the bed and put it to one side on a wall of earth. It was to be seen standing there for a long time, amid the building framework, the cranes, the piles of lumber and tar pots, soon it was overlaid by a thick layer of dust and mortar, which the ferryman brushed away every night as best he could. The ferryman's new shack was already standing down on the riverbank, yet he spent the night up above out in the open next to his son's sleeping-place, leaned on the edge of the bed, his legs drawn up to his body. The high buildings grew, the bed with the recumbent one on it was shoved here and there, and often it was banged or run into hard, the legs were broken off, only the mattress still held together, and there lay Jum wrapped in his blanket, and could look up at the windows of the telegraph office, out of which the lady telegraphists, just moved in, threw him kisses. For they, too, soon loved him, they loved the shining full moon of his face and his round belly showing itself under the blanket, and during their coffee breaks they brought him coffee and cakes. And the impression arose, according to the ferryman's description, that the bed is still there, among the big buildings, perhaps behind the service-truck garage, on the courtyard level, from which point the cupola skylight windows rise up at regular intervals.

I lived in this house on the fifth story at the time the office in the top story was being set up. Mostly I lay in bed, stretched out flat on my back, and only occasionally went to the broad window, to the table with the glass top, and looked out onto the playgrounds, repair shops and bus stops. Mornings, half-awake, I often saw a field in my mind's eye before me, brightly lit by the sun, I saw every blade of grass, with clover, poppies, cuckoo-flowers among it, the smell was there and I scented it in the wind, I held fast to this image, slowly I soared along with it, until other images came, there I was lying under boards and pulpy cardboard at the edge of the river, in front of the railroad bridge, and saw the nightly manifestations and the manifestations of the daytime, and whatever showed itself was unclear and only illusion, and the only actuality was a hand, or a foot, and this limb thrust itself through the thin wall that surrounded me and forced its way in, and it was covered with stiff hairs, it was part of no body, it was an independent organism, it crept up to me in a place where the air was sticky and viscid, and then I saw that already this space was filled with masses of the same kind of moving things, big feet, hands, rumps and necks, all covered with hair and scurfy, many with mouths mutely opening and closing, there were also rows of teeth with tatters of flesh on them, and half-ears in the bloody encrustations of which gold glittered, and fingers with jewels embedded right in them, and all this moved under me, and it was up to me to find out what kind of puddle, pit this was, and sometimes I got as far as my pile of boards, for long intervals felt safely hidden in my lair, or I pushed my way even as far as my bed, on which I lay flat, capable of no other movement except to bore into my nose, than to twist my head to one side and cast a look outside at the new buildings, then the other thing was there again and this time it began with a sucking, my mouth still sucked itself tightly shut and then was torn away, or that on which it had been sucking was torn away, spittle ran out of my mouth, and there were lips to be seen, strained wide open, with wet teeth inside and a tongue stretched out that made twisting movements, yet out of this mouth blood was already gushing and the bleeding mouth crept back over small heads of cabbage thickly planted together, over burst skulls, set in rows in a field, and they all snapped with little mouths and opened and closed little eyes, and each face was formed

in its own special way, with special skin blemishes,
summer freckles, with a scar, a dimple, a pair of steel
specs. I made a superhuman effort to explain all this to
myself, and doing it thought about a white sheet of paper the emptiness of which could be completely filled
up with words, and I heard myself babble, babble all
a-dabble scrabble gabble rabble fabble, dame came
name lame fame same, taste paste haste waste, hand
sand land, sing spring, wind sinned, think stink sink
dink wink pink rinkydinky finky, donkey tonky, piss
hiss niche witch bitch ditch turn spurn earn learn see
pee mow go hickerydickery slithermithery hoppetyho,
but these or similar words eluded me, covered nothing
up at all, I could only make this lalling and babbling, it
was all taken up, this mass of words, by one perception,
yet this perception was only that I understood nothing,
could explain nothing, and all that I wanted was to sim-
plify my situation, well then, I thought, I have run away
from my wife and my children have been dashed
against the wall, they have probably flung me into a jail
and then, as they usually do, into a mass grave, and now
I must bear witness, give reckoning, for a life with all
its ways run and left behind, all doors opened and
closed, all its movements and its touchings, its words,
that flood of words uttered and taken in, to no other
end than to have them trickle away, melt into a blur,
come to nothing. And there I lay, among the fragmen-
tations creeping all about, amid this overflowing mass
of limbs all soundlessly opening and closing their

mouths, and each mouth was a bloodied hole, and over it all grew hair, and nails sprouted on the wandering fingers and toes, and far above us, on hard-trampled ground which had been replanted with grass and shrubs, that was where the sounds came from, and when I strove even more I could hear how up above it was cracking and crunching and how at the same time there was a singing and whistling, and then I burrowed my way upward, although that is really impossible, and got to a point somewhere in front of this field, these grasses, this wind, lay a long time under piles of boards, until in the spring the snow melted and the ground opened up in many places in small, perfectly round craters, and out of each an arm stuck up, a foot, a head with an open mouth, and it was hair that was waving among the grasses. Thus I lay, as the attic story over me was renovated, sucked on my fingers, turned my head toward the window, imagined myself a meadow in the wind and also became active again, too, and bestirred myself, despite my supposed fatigue, to get up and out. An ordinary morning, with the sounds of people working. I woke up to a brief burst of ringing on the phone. When I took the receiver off the hook nothing but a scratching and a crackling were to be heard, then the connection went dead. I put on my bathrobe and went to the apartment door in slippers, my pajama pants, which were too big for me, and which I held together about my body. In the stairwell painters were standing on ladders and with jets of flame from their blow-

torches were scorching paint off the walls, the layers of
paint bubbled and boiled, blew up into fat blisters and
curled in brown flaps about the scraping putty-knives.
The flames had strayed over the wires which hung bare
on the wall and which led to a junction box over my
door, I pointed up at them with my finger and said they
had been burnt out, and what I said was not intelligible
in the harsh sizzling. I climbed a couple of rungs up a
ladder and screamed my complaint into the roaring
and was told that I would have to talk to the foreman.
Holding to my pants tight I went down between the
scaffolding and the heaps of charred paint-bark, down
the stairs to the newly built rooms in which employees
were already putting papers and volumes of documents into cabinets and onto shelves, and carrying
chairs, desks, typewriters and adding machines here
and there. I called for the foreman and the cry echoed
strangely in my own ears. In the corridor a linoleum
runner was being stretched out and fastened down, I
had to jump over the roll as it came my way and doing
so lost a slipper. I bent down to look for the slipper, but
could not find it among the cardboard boxes filled with
printed matter and clerical equipment, was also ham-
pered by the pajama pants which kept slipping down.
I asked a couple of secretaries who were carrying a
swivel-chair by me where the foreman was, and they
only looked at me with eyebrows raised. I rubbed the
sleep out of my eyes and went on, one foot slippered
the other naked, and came into a room in which men

in white smocks were standing at a table looking down over blueprints spread out. I asked them for the foreman, they turned to me and looked me over, and when I explained to them that my phone wires in the stairwell had been destroyed, all that they said, while looking at my naked foot and the hand I kept under the bathrobe to hold up my pants, was that it had nothing to do with them. I made it known to them that I had suffered a substantial loss through the loss of my phone connection, that I did most of my business over the phone. I lived from selling books, was an agent for horticultural publications, expensive works on the art of cookery, horticulture and infant care, and during the forenoon hours carried on conversations with people who, the evening before, I had carefully selected from the phone book according to a certain system, and told them how good the books were and how attractive the purchase terms. After this explanation the building bosses directed me to a phone company man who was supposed to be busy somewhere in the entrance hall. Two employees carrying in a green fireproof strongbox pushed me to one side, and I again went out into the corridor to look for the phone company man. I called out for him and again became aware of the strange sound of my voice and then I spied him behind a glass partition, installing a switchboard. He turned his face up to me, his forehead was wrinkled, and between his lips he held a series of screws and plugs. He directed me to the main office and got busy again with the vari-colored phone cable wires that had been separated and stuck up in bundles out of the switchboard. I turned about and went back down the corridor, where once again I rummaged among the boxes and office furniture in search of my lost slipper. An older woman, possibly a bookkeeper or cashier, asked me what I was looking for. I replied that while in search of someone whom I could make responsible for the damage done to my phone connection, my slipper, as I was jumping over the roll of linoleum runner, had fallen from my foot, and she promised, in a soothing tone, that soon new phone services would be installed, and my slipper, if it was found, would be returned to me, something that brought tears to my eyes, and so I went back to my room, where I took the path of least resistance and waited for the day to pass.

And once we were riding in a coach, drawn by a runaway horse, the reins were broken, the coachman had fallen off the seat, round the square stormed the horse until in front of the hotel in which the room was all ready and waiting for us the porter and houseman, as well as a couple of policemen who had come hurrying up, grabbed hold of the harness straps and brought the horse to a standstill. While the redly speckled horse was rearing up and snuffing and throwing his head back, the big door was held open ahead of us, we walked up on red carpeting, the door to the room was opened and then shut again behind us, at the sides of the open balcony window the drapes fluttered, and outside lay the city, oh this city, which we had never seen, those buildings in yellow ochre, those green roofs, that sky of inimitable blue. Similarly, now, we had ridden through a snowstorm, and now warmth streamed toward us, dry sandy salty warmth. And although we had spent a year, perhaps seven years, with one another, it was as if we were touching each other for the first time. After a long separation, a long separation we stripped off each other's clothes from our skin, and our eyes were wide open so as to see each other's every movement, and her face was white, white as the walls of the room, and her teeth glittered as if she were laughing about something inconceivably amazing, and so we breathed on one another, and from outdoors this light came piercing in, a light that we knew from no dream. Oh, this changed city, these hours of reunion after forgotten days and nights, these hours until dawn when she had become so attenuated that I hardly saw her any more, only felt her, on my knees, her face could still be faintly seen, her arms lay about my neck, yet she was lifeless, or sunken into deep sleep, only once did her eyelids move slightly, they lifted just a crack only to close again, and when the cock crowed on the balcony under our window she had vanished, it had become light, it had become blindingly light, she had vanished, yet I still felt her, in the flat of my hand, and there, too, where my other hand was missing I felt her, her skin, her hair, yet the city outside already again was as it always was, as it always was.

The house into which my father went, this big white house with many windows, its walls covered with slabs of white stone, I do not know how I should describe this house, whether it should be called beautiful or ugly, or whether within it could be lived in at all. Every single piece of stone facing is screwed fast into the wall decoration at the four corners, the stone is shot through with bluish veins, there is copper flashing at each window frame. This facade is there to show wealth, many stones, many windows, so many that I cannot count them, and yet at one time they were nevertheless counted. Marble and copper, on and on we walk past this facade, along past these countless windows, these countless white slabs of stone. There he comes again out of the big front door, he is walking stiff and straight, hands in the pockets of his topcoat and the heels of his shoes click in regular beat on the sidewalk. Perhaps he is taking a walk after the day's work, he is going the rounds of his property, enjoying the evening air, looking up proudly at the gigantic white block, at this factory, this world-girdling business house, this work of a lifetime, he breathes in deeply, he is still in full possession of his powers, comes back in again through the entrance, rides upstairs on the chair-elevator, sticks the key from the bunch of keys into the keyhole of the door, turns the key, presses down the latch, goes into the hallway, making noises which always make an impression on his children in the depths of the apartment. Yet it seems to me his topcoat is shabby and the heels of his shoes worn down. Perhaps he is only the doorkeeper here. His shoulders are weary, his head is sunken down, he takes his hands out of his pockets and they dangle limply at his sides. Yes, my father was always worried, was always ready to be put upon and upbraided, he had never made it beyond night porter, for days on end he probably had never dared ask house visitors what it might be they wanted, timidly he walked across the courtyard, perhaps to take care of the furnace, or unloaded the firewood, and only at night could he sit at the window of his cubby at the entrance-way, behind double-barred gratings. We lived in lodgings, in a couple of small rooms, and certainly it was not in this house, but in another smaller older one. Nights from my bed, through the glass door, in the panes of which a couple of bent tulip stems were cut, I could see my father on the chair near his dormer window, hours on end I saw his face, which he kept tensely turned toward the gate and his hand lay ready on the alarm-bell button, yet never, never did he press the button and the bell did not sound, and my brothers lay in their beds and slept, and in the adjoining room my mother snored. I know how every night I struggled against the impulse to go out there to him, who sat there so mutely, and once I did it perhaps, for it seems to me as if I can remember seeing how his face crinkled into a smile, and how for a moment he took his hand from the bell button and stroked me on my forehead. This moment often comes back to me, at night in some street or other, or when I am going down the stairs in some house or other then it is as if I were going downstairs here, and right away

I am off into nowhere, a great span of time behind me and before me a great span of time, and at this moment just a couple of steps in a street or on some stairs or other and presto I have vanished into this other world.

And now I see the ferryman's house, as it looked at that time, when I had climbed up one evening from the riverbank. It was a small house, made of planks painted dark red and with white corner-posts and blue window frames. The ferryman had come up after the day's work, he had closed the garden gate behind him and had gone along the path to the door of the house. From the field where a couple of cows were grazing came a woman with a milk pail, she was a thin, dark-haired woman with a knot of black hair at the nape of her neck. She went into the house without looking to right or left, and yet he was standing only a couple of steps away from her. He took the small stubby pipe he had been smoking out of his mouth, knocked it out on the stone steps in front of the door and stuck it in his pocket. He stood for a long time at the door and solitary sounds came up from the city and a cow mooed from the meadow. Then he went into the house, and for a long time nothing happened, I sat at the edge of the road and nobody came by, and in the house it was quiet and a bird with long red tail-feathers flew over and from far away came some sort of bang. Suddenly the woman ran out of the door with her skirt flying and her hair waving loose behind her, she ran to the barn with big bounds unhindered by her heavy shoes and the ferryman came rushing out of the door behind her, his knee buckled as he hit the ground, yet he got up and flew after her and both disappeared into the barn. Again it was still for a long time, I ducked down low in the leafiness at the fence and held my breath, and then I saw a gigantic figure emerge from the house, a man with a naked hairy torso and long reddish brown hair on his head braided into braids at the side, with a wildly growing beard, with tremendously knotty arms, the skin of them overrun with tattoos, wearing boots that reached over his knees and which had the tops turned down and spurs at the heels. He opened his mouth wide and in the dark cavern single yellow teeth could be seen, he pumped his chest full of air, and I waited for his outcry, yet everything stayed still, he just stood there, with his powerful gaping, and slowly turned round and went back into the house. And I crept down the road and ran breathlessly along the path on the riverbank, here, where streets have now been built, bridges and underpinnings for wharves, here where we are walking now, where we are walking walking walking